BLACK GATE TALES

PAUL DRAPER

Cover and all illustrations by the brilliant Phillip Kingsbury at Wooden Spoon Press: www.woodenspoonpress.com

Edited by Robert Grossmith: www.robertgrossmith.com

FIRST EDITION

ISBN 978-1-9996630-1-8 (paperback)
ISBN 978-1-9996630-0-1 (ebook)

www.theblackgate.co.uk

CONTENTS

Preface

I now live in Bournemouth, England.

Beyond the wealth and show of south coast life lies a deeply soulful landscape. From the shingle of the Jurassic Coast along to monolithic Hengistbury Head and up through the oaks and pines of the New Forest, it's as arcane and witchy a place as any other in the British Isles and, if you're quiet and watch what nature does, just as unfathomable and ancient.

I haven't lived here all my life. I was born and grew up in Suffolk and drank in its lore and history as a boy. These stories are suffused with imaginations and ponderings as much from those times as from now, derived from nightly walks on the heath with my good friend Taff, from trips to the old coast of Felixstowe and time spent watching the River Orwell slip and toil through its estuary. Black Shuck roams that county.

The most directly connected story here is *Snick*. Tolmere Heath is my version of Rushmere Heath; a place of impenetrable gorse and bracken, a place a boy could pedal his bike along dirt tracks until his thighs burned, before stopping and wondering what that noise was just beyond the tree line.

After leaving Suffolk at 21, I drank in the works of Arthur Machen, J.S. le Fanu, M.R. James, H.P. Lovecraft, Algernon Blackwood, William Hope Hodgson and all those long-passed masters of the cosmic weird.

So here you have a collision of all these things.

I hope you enjoy them.

Paul Draper, Bournemouth
18th December 2020

And something born of the snowy desolation, born of the midnight and the silent grandeur, born of the great listening hollows of the night, something that lay 'twixt terror and wonder, dropped from the vast wintry spaces down into his heart—and called him.

Algernon Blackwood,
The Glamour of the Snow

The Wrong Harvest

"Boy! Stop! Stop!"

I look at the bird who so rudely called. A typical crow; ill-mannered and haughty.

"Why?" I ask. He fixes me from the top branch with a glassy eye, head still, and just repeats himself. I lay the rune-stone on the stile and walk on.

The summer light is fading. The bronze rays thread sharply through the trees as the Earth rotates away from the day. I still have plenty of ground to cover and head through the woods at the south end of the farm.

Two weeks before, I'd nearly turned away from Mrs Greenhalgh's house, but I saw the curtain move and felt eyes upon me, so I pushed through the chipped gate and walked up the path.

"Come in, she's in the kitchen." Old Mr Greenhalgh looked down at me from behind his glasses, owlish and impassive.

I went down the hall, past bronze figurines and fading white china plates. I passed a dried lemon perched on the windowsill, with nails tacked into it, and rowan loops threaded around the banister. At the end of the passage a thin, white-painted wooden door opened to a small, stone-flagged kitchen. Mrs Greenhalgh sat at the table with her back to me, watching the birds in a sparsely branched cherry tree beyond the window. Turning, she looked younger than I remembered her, but her hair was grey and hung loosely around her slender face.

"You should have come before now," she said.

"I..."

"Sit down. We have a fair bit to discuss."

I sat, and she poured tea.

The woods carry on for about half a mile and eventually break to reveal the perimeter of the lower fallow field. Such fields sing in low voices to my ears, as kin-species of crop harmonise at the rise and fall of the day.

The fallow field is different. Across it span various grasses and sedges, each with their own whispering melody. Wild flowers punctuate the grass and spike and chime intermittently. On a quiet day I can catch the low reverberation of worms and insects in the ground; deep bass notes beneath soil and root.

The fallow field is quieter than it should be. Not much light falls here; the high woods to the south block the sunlight, the oaks having grown high and thick.

I place another stone by the gap in the hawthorn hedge

and walk through. A spider thanks me in passing for not disturbing its fledgling web.

I drank Mrs Greenhalgh's sweet tea and, as she spoke, I felt the tension drop from my shoulders.

"You're what, sixteen?"

"Yes. School finished last month."

"So, tell me what you know."

I braced myself. Then the words tumbled out. Mum leaving without saying goodbye, my sister going away, the young foreign people we'd had help around the house who never stayed, my father's rage...

My father's hollow eyes.

"You have something of his?"

I put the old wallet I'd brought with me on the table.

She picked it up and nodded. "Come back tomorrow."

I walk on along the public footpath running up the side of the hedgerow. Starlings wheel and call out from the sky, but they're too high to be understood. The patchwork of crops separates me from the farmhouse, which stands unlit in the gathering dusk.

I move alongside the wheat field. We sprayed it last month, and the still-green stalks stand stiff and mature. Next month they'll be harvested, and the cycle begins again. For now, they sway in waves on the steady breeze, and their choral tone reaches my ears.

I take a few minutes at a ditch to catch my breath. Long hours in the studio with paint and canvas have eroded my fitness. A tiny muttering arises from the wheat. A field mouse.

"You should leave," the small voice says. "Don't carry on."

I turn the third runestone over in my hands, my eyes hunting for the thing. "Why? What's the problem?"

For a minute, it's just the scrape of sliding wheat leaves brushing one another in the wind. "They should stay put," says the unseen mouse. The voice tails off as it darts further into the field.

When I returned, Mrs Greenhalgh's face was stony and tired. We went into her garden to talk.

"Your father is a dark man." She looked me in the eye. "He's the reason so many people have left this town, including your mother. It's in the sticks and dice." She tailed off and frowned. "I…can't see everything."

"I hear things," I said, fumbling for a way to explain.

"Yes, that's about you. What do you hear?"

"It used to be just music, but there are voices now. Everywhere on the farm. Sometimes warnings, but never specific."

Mrs Greenhalgh tutted, walked over to her cherry tree and ran her hand along the smooth bark. "Animals never get to the point, but nature can know what we don't. I'll give you some runestones. I want you to set them around the perimeter of the farm as I work here. This is a powerful old trick and should reveal more. Your farm is astride a particular ley, and that energy will combine with the stones. Do it as night approaches, next Tuesday fort-night. Lay the last stone at 9pm, understood?"

I nodded and left with a laden bag.

The last stone is for the wall west of the oilseed rape field. A couple of months ago it was blazing with yellow flowers, but now the field is a dull brown, ready for the harvest.

I check my watch as I approach the western boundary wall. It's 8:55pm. Over at the farmhouse the porch light comes on. Dad would settle in now, beer bottle open.

The light is fading. I place the last stone on the wall.

Five minutes pass. A song thrush lands on the wall beside me.

"It is done. They're coming," it says, head cocked.

I stare at it.

"They're coming. The fallow field."

My throat tightens. The gloaming is here, and the moon bright in the sky, but I can't see the lower field from the wall. I jump off and run to the footpath by the wheat field's edge. I look down the hill, towards that meadow and the black woods beyond.

Shapes approach in the gloom. They shamble and lope.

I back away amongst the wheat stalks. Turning, I run towards the house, but the going is heavy across the ruts, and the crop is thick. My foot lands askew, ankle twisting. I cry with pain, falling to the dirt.

"Shh!" says a familiar little voice. Tiny eyes glint in the moonlight. "Don't move! Be still!"

Stalks get crushed just yards away. Something is pushing into the field. I lay still on my back, trying not to breathe.

Dark figures pass slowly over and around me.

I count eight, but hear more on either side. They are slender and tattered of flesh, eye sockets crammed with soil. They shamble through the warm dusk air towards the farmhouse. I listen hard, but of all the life I hear about me, the cacophony of plants and animals my gift allows, I hear nothing from these figures, just the tread and stumble of footfall. They are empty.

The last figure has a gold bracelet I recognise from childhood. I used to play with it when she cuddled me, telling me not to worry about the wind in the fields at night, or the far-off screech of the owl. Tears fill my eyes as the hideous, blighted shape stumbles onwards.

"Go now!" whispers the little voice. I clamber to my feet and hobble away as fast as I can.

This is the hour none living should see, the hour of a price paid.

As I reach the driveway I hear the splintering of the farmhouse door, and keep going.

Mrs Pendleton's Corpse

IN WHICH A VILLAGE UNDERTAKER IS AWOKEN
IN THE NIGHT BY AN UNEXPECTED DEMAND.

My beloved wife Jane remained
ill. Her cough, rattling and
raspy, had driven her to bed the
previous week. The curtains
were drawn on the view of the
rooftops of our little English
village. Her pain worsened by
the day.

One night she insisted with
a wave that it was "too hot" for me to lie alongside her. I
relocated to the guest room with thoughts of a better rest.
Our walls were thin, however, and I could still hear her
wheezing as I waited for sleep.

Another sound drifted over this, like the wailing of a
cat. Half in slumber, I couldn't tell where it came from—
only that it rose from downstairs. I donned my slippers and
crept along the hall and down into the funeral parlour.

Still the sound came from downstairs.

Odd, as that should have been the quietest room of all.

I turned on the light and shuffled past the familiar

workplace objects; coffin wood samples, brass handle displays, embossed marble gravestones. Down through the sealed door, into the cold room.

THERE YOU ARE.

"Hello?" I ventured, shivering slightly.

HERE.

One table was bare, having been recently vacated by Stanley Burrows, a kindly baker who had succumbed to pneumonia last week. A sheet covered the other table, under which lay old Mrs Pendleton. I drew it back to reveal her small and lifeless face, eyes obscured by lace.

I'VE LOOKED BETTER, I KNOW.

"Mrs Pendleton?"

YES. I NEED TO BE BURIED BY DAWN.

I am a man of steady blood, as those in our vocation need to be. Many kinds of corpse come through our parlours, some in a violent shape. A talking one was a first.

The carriage had brought Mrs Pendleton to us only yesterday morning. She had been found sprawled dead across a hedge at the bottom of her garden by a shocked postman. She lived high on the hill and the villagers avoided her. She was the longest-living resident of the place. In her garden there grew only thorns and agonised trees with coal-black berries.

This was the most she had spoken to me since my time in the village.

I took stock. I hadn't been drinking (I do not drink), I was awake and to my knowledge not suffering a fever. Being thus intact, it seemed only polite to continue the conversation.

"Why is that?" I offered.

IT'S COMPLICATED. YOU WOULDN'T UNDER-STAND. Her mouth didn't move as she spoke the papery and sibilant words. If an adder in a hedgerow could talk, it might sound similar.

"Well, it's impossible, I'm afraid. I need to prepare you," I said.

BEFORE SUNRISE.

"But we have a service scheduled for Thursday."

IF I AM NOT IN THE GROUND BY DAWN, I WON'T LEAVE YOU. IF I AM, I WILL OFFER YOU A GIFT.

I am not fond of unreasonable and demanding people, neither alive nor dead, so I left Mrs Pendleton and returned to bed.

～

I lay down and closed my eyes.

IT'LL BE LIKE THIS, she said in the dark, as clearly and loudly as when I had stood next to her. For the next twenty minutes she chatted about the most banal of topics; juniper bush care, feeding times for her many cats and the unacceptable rising price of bread since the war.

It was insufferable. Within the hour I found myself walking through the moonlit village with a hessian sack on my back, the gossamer-light remains of old Mrs Pendleton within.

The night was silent and the leaves in the trees remained untroubled by wind.

I made for the cemetery. The digger, Mr Kendall, had been working on a couple of plots over the weekend. One would suffice, if dug a little deeper and re-covered using a shovel from his undefended tool shed.

THIS WON'T WORK, said Mrs Pendleton, continuing her annoying running commentary.

"It's a cemetery," I replied, "it's where you were headed anyway."

HE WON'T LET THE LIKES OF ME IN THERE.

We arrived at the wall of St Michael's Church. I pushed open the rusty gate and crept in along the moonlit path. It was then that an invisible force like a giant's fist slammed against my shoulder and tore the sack from my grasp. As I spun under the blow, I saw it hurled thirty yards back away through the gate. The sack bounced before sliding to a ghastly rest against the kerb.

I DID SAY.

I gave it two more goes before abandoning the attempt, and each time the unseen force wrenched away the sack. Mrs Pendleton was being rejected by the very fabric of the churchyard, like a barn owl throwing a pellet up and out of its gullet.

I looked up at the church steeple framed against the moon. The old stone gargoyles gazed down.

I'M NOT REALLY HIS TYPE.

"Yes, I think we can conclude that."

I went back in alone to pick up a shovel before returning.

We walked on, away from the village centre and towards the heath. It was 4:30am according to my watch.

Leaving the road, we wound our way through the gorse bushes and across the grassy plain towards Blackthorn Wood. I recalled a ragged, sandy scar on the heath called Devil's Trough. The soil there should take a spade.

CAN YOU GO A BIT FASTER?

I gave that the frosty silence it deserved.

I WAS CARELESS, REALLY.

"What do you mean?"

PASSING AWAY.

"Well, we all die."

I MISSED THE CROW RITUAL. FORGETFUL THESE DAYS.

I had no idea what she was talking about and walked on. Along the way, she spoke about how her days had affected the harvest, producing tinctures for revenge or for passion, and how nobody seemed to want her services any more, not even to dispatch a rival lover.

We soon arrived at Devil's Trough.

I'M SCEPTICAL TO BE HONEST.

"Well, it'll have to do. We have an hour before dawn."

I started digging, and the spade made simple work of the sand. Clouds drifted across the moon and ground faded from sight a little. When the moonlight returned, I saw that small figures surrounded us.

MOVE SLOWLY, said Mrs Pendleton from her bundled position on the pathway.

I peered at the little forms, no higher than my knee. They seemed neither animal, plant, nor human, and were covered with a gritty carapace, like the dusty shell of maggots. Some had a single eye, and some had many. All looked hostile.

GO SLOW OR THEY'LL HAVE THE SKIN FROM YOUR BACK. THIS IS OLD GROUND. STANDING STONES WERE HERE, ONCE.

I nudged some of the soil I had moved back into the fledgling grave. At this, the closest figure moved its head slightly. I backed away, being watched all the time. When I had retreated to Mrs Pendleton, the figures crowded around, kicking the earth back into the hole. Within a moment, they were gone.

We had forty minutes left until dawn.

I hurried with Mrs Pendleton towards the woods.

"Folks don't seem to like you much, do they?"

IT COMES WITH THE JOB.

I didn't want to know more. I just wanted to go back to bed and be done with this night.

Sunrise approached as we reached the middle of the small wood.

THIS SHOULD DO.

"I should hope so," I said. "You're not heavy, but my back is complaining."

I COULD HAVE GIVEN YOU SOMETHING FOR THAT.

She mumbled on as I dug. The ground was hard and compacted, but after a time I had fashioned a shallow grave.

CAN I KEEP THE SACK? IT'S NICE.

It certainly would not be used for vegetables again. I lowered it into the hole and covered it with a yard of soil.

THANK YOU. I AM GIVING YOU A GIFT, AS I PROMISED.

"Really, no need. It's my job. Although not like this most of the time."

IT IS DONE.

After these words I heard no more from old Mrs Pendleton.

The sun rose as I left the place, and to my knowledge she lies in Blackthorn Wood to this day, covered by winding grass.

I returned home and arrived to a broken heart.

Jane had died. I found her on the floor by her bed, eyes wide open and spittle on her lips. I had no idea that her worsening condition had been that serious, and wept for a day.

My apprentice took on preparing her, something I could not do. The house was unbearable and silent, there was so much left to say.

On the third night, as I lay awake wondering about Mrs Pendleton and her gift, I heard Jane's voice as clearly as it had sounded on the day I'd met her.

I'M STILL HERE.

With Love, a Meal

The farmhouse kitchen is well-equipped and warm, with a wide bay window looking out upon the large and darkening garden. Sandra peers out. There they are again, in the approaching dusk; the shapes of her children. She taps on the glass.

"Dinner!" she calls. No one can hear through the window, but the tap and wave are long-established signals. Soon it will be time to eat together.

Sandra is preparing the meal the same way she has for years; creating a fresh salad bar to wheel over to the family table. Her routine is well-rehearsed and methodical. Most of the vegetables and fruits are homegrown, a rich summer bounty of verdant shapes and succulent smells.

She brings the ingredients from the larder, fetches dressing from the fridge, and prepares.

Tomatoes. The slicing knife is sharp and her grip is firm, fingers pinched. Sandra remembers the tight metal umbilical clamp in the delivery room, after baby Esme had struggled her way into the world. She recalled the heat of the receding pain, how that small clip gripped across the cord. The obstetrician's scissors were blunt-looking, but they did the job. The cord dropped like a snake shot from a tree. This kitchen blade glides through the red tomato skins. The cut is clean.

Cucumber. Stiff and green, again sliced. The discs stack like little plates as she lines the serving bowl on the bar. They look like checkers. One of her son Scott's favourite games was Connect Four; they played it with little yellow and red discs that dropped with a plastic click into a matrix frame. She had loved those summer afternoons playing with Scott, even when he wouldn't sit still. Between six and eight years of age he seemed to be perpetually upside down or jumping about like a flea. His silliness always made her laugh. She thinks of his head resting on her lap as his energy went from 100 percent to zero in seconds. She smiles as she slices.

Lettuce. Sandra washes the bright green leaves and shakes them onto the counter. Droplets fly like spray from a car's wheels. She starts to chop. The click-clack of the knife makes quick work of the dense heads. She leaves some larger leaves unchopped, creating little nests on the salad bar trolley that she will place the other items upon. They look like the shells of elfin scallops. It reminds Sandra of Lauren and the shell-patterned green prom dress she wore at the end of her school days. She was a beautiful girl and had her father Derek's eyes; the palest green. She gripped secrets behind those eyes. Sandra had watched Lauren grow up and grow away, emotions unbridled, fiercely uncertain of the things she shouted down the stairwell before she left.

Sweetcorn. Sandra takes the sweetcorn off the boil and places it in dishes. The cobs are weighty and steaming, the yellow surfaces bumpy. Butter fresh from the fridge slides down the sides, as moisture curls above. The family always likes the cob whole and, besides, dividing them is an odious, tough task. Derek used to do it though, his rough hands making simple work of cleaving the cylindrical pith. Sandra recalls the gentle crush of those arms and the bass rumble of his voice as her ear pressed against his chest in the darkness.

She tries not to think of that phone call. The agony wept into the carpet.

Sandra wheels the salad bar to the table and sets the placemats around a centrepiece vase of roses. Their sweet scent gilds the air.

She looks out of the bay window. Of course, the children didn't come in. The darkness frames their shapes, and once again they look like what they are, a row of small hawthorn trees with branches set against the ancient stars.

Sandra's fingers are old. The pale, liver-spotted skin on her hands stretches and corrugates as she serves water to each place. She puts a portion of salad on her own plate and raises a glass to the room. She eats slowly, appreciating each morsel across a tongue less sensitive than the one that used to savour ice creams on the boardwalk on cool summer evenings.

A carriage clock marks the half hour.

All the chairs but hers are empty. The gradual, powerful impact of past years has left the farmhouse pregnant with a thousand silent memories. Preparing the food as she used to helps to calm her ghosts before she sleeps.

Sandra clears her plate away, turns off the light, and

climbs the stairs. She passes the window looking out to where his car once was.

She dons her favourite white-ribboned nightgown and, before long, drifts off to sleep.

Once again the farmhouse fills with voices.

The Puppeteer of Prague

It was the first day of March 1939, but Prague was as cold as the heart of winter.

After leaving the half-empty office, I was too distraught to go home and face Marie, so I crossed the Old Town Square to Pavel's Bar and drank. I couldn't understand how things had become this bad.

After a time, Pavel pushed me towards the door, saying, "Jiří, you have done what you can. What will be, will be. Please, go home."

I swayed out into the night air and ignored the whooping, black-shirted university goons gathering under the towering Gothic steeples of the Týnský chrám. I wanted nothing to do with them.

My hazy stumbling led me to a little cobbled alley, with stones shiny in the moonlight. The alley was dark, except for an illuminated bar sign halfway down. Marie would be long in bed by now, so I wandered through the door and found myself in an unfamiliar place, talking to an unfamiliar face.

The bartender introduced himself as Vaclav and poured us both some steaming svařák. The lighting was low. Hushed figures sat at tables around us.

"Thank you," I said.

"Friend, you are welcome," he replied. "You would think we are at Christmas. I cannot see from my windows in the morning for frost." He was a small man, in his fifties, but his eyes were alive with a youthful energy. He was bearded, wore a dark blue corduroy jacket, and sported a peaked cap atop a mass of hair. "Your face is full of sadness. Tell me why."

I heaved a sigh. Pavel's beer was tripping my tongue, and the words took time to form. "We are about to fall to Hitler, it is a matter of time. Hacha is to travel to Berlin within a week or two. It's over."

"Ah," replied Vaclav. "Don't be so sure."

"What can we do? The Sudetenland was supposed to be the end. As it is, we have fed meat to wolves, and the pack is hungry for more. Hacha will be a puppet or gone by the end of spring."

Vaclav tilted his glass and watched the steam rise into the half-light. "A puppet maybe, but do not underestimate the power of such. Let me tell you a tale that may give you heart."

And so he began.

~

The puppeteer drew the crowds. He was an excellent performer. Each Friday night on his stage, in an auditorium between the Charles Bridge and the castle, he would present his marionettes to applause and laughter. We Czechs love our puppets.

He had a wide range of characters in his black travelling case, which was almost as tall as himself. He would arrive on stage stern-faced, and flick the ornate silver clasps open as the hubbub of the audience lowered with the lights.

Out they would come! The tales they would tell. Poor Peter and Gretel, lost in the woods and menaced by a wild bear. Then Felicia Du Mornay, a baroness from England, woeful in her tales of jewel-encrusted misery, and blinded by the wonders she lived alongside. Lastly, there was the main star...Lord Gustav.

Gustav was top-hatted and monocled, with an air of authority. Made from pale linden, he would stroll with his cane across the stage in an uncanny gait, his long coat swirling about his fine boots. The secret of puppetry is not yanking the wooden controller, it is the touching of the strings, and this puppeteer was a master. As Gustav walked, the puppeteer slid his free hand along the strings, slowly and softly, and each twitch produced a lifelike movement from Gustav. The lord peered into the crowd. He told them about his life as a respectable noble, then conducted interviews with those in the audience, small wooden hands crossed behind his back. It was eerie. A person sitting seven rows back could tell precisely if Lord Gustav's painted eyes were looking straight at him. After initial embarrassment the audience member would start talking to Gustav as if he were human.

And for that moment, he was.

These were mixed audiences. There were soldiers, market sellers, traders and artisans. There were young lovers on dates, and older folks out to forget their troubles and find some laughter. For this was not so long ago. These times were the same troubling times we find ourselves in now.

Every so often government officials would be in the audience. These were the people preparing Czechoslovakia for its dark fate from the north. Gustav found these people fascinating. He would step closer, the spotlight swinging his way as he strolled along the ground towards the interviewee. The interrogation was both funny and deep.

"So," Gustav intoned one night. "You work for the Interior Ministry?" He cocked his head to one side as the crowd looked on in amazement.

"Yes, yes I do," chortled the fat and moustachioed gentleman. "Twenty-two years this summer."

"I see, and you conduct this work in the restaurant?" said Gustav, cane pointed at the man's belly.

The gentleman was good-humoured and took this with a chuckle. "Yes, I suppose you could say that!"

"We find ourselves in trying times," said Gustav, tapping his cane on the ground.

"We do, but what will be will be."

Gustav swept a hand across his brow in feigned shock and the audience roared.

Later that evening a mist descended across Charles Bridge and hung in the air above the ground. The statues were half-hidden on the ornate rails, and beside the walkway rows of stony legs pushed up through the fog, supporting unseen bodies. The fat and moustachioed man hurried across, the warmth of the night's beer not sufficient to ward away eager thoughts of a pan-heated bed.

There came a tapping sound, wood on stone. The

man stopped and peered around. Seeing nothing, he continued, but halted again at a rat-a-tat-tat.

"Anyone there, bedevil?" he called.

No answer came, but from the height of a fog-shrouded statue a tiny, long-coated figure lowered itself.

"What the--?" spluttered the man, rubbing his eyes.

The figure tapped a stick on the side of the statue and the man walked closer.

It was Lord Gustav, head cocked to one side.

The fat man's body now sways in the cold currents of the Vltava. It is raw and pale, and the fish take a little more away each day.

Vaclav's words washed over me like a dream. I absorbed each one as he told his story, but the wine and the shadowy atmosphere of the bar had woven a paralysing spell across me. His voice had a sonorous, bass quality and in my stupor it sounded like the intonation of a calming oracle.

"You see," he said, "puppets can be influential in the right circumstances. Have some more wine."

He poured, and the svařák swirled in the glass, misting the sides and condensing in little clouds above it.

"And yet, there is more. These things did not end atop Charles Bridge that night."

He continued his tale.

Prague is an old city. It was a tribal intersection before the various Roman Empires, both Holy and unholy, made it such an important trading base. The cold, coursing artery of the Vltava has carried life to the city, but also sometimes destruction. It was the capital of Bohemia before it was our nation, and the allies of the Habsburgs marched across these same narrow streets. I wonder where their feet fell -- perhaps you do too? Prague is a monolith of power, but also something alive. It is my view that God himself lives in this city, somewhere across the crooked rooftops and garrets. Perhaps as a cat, perhaps just on the cold air that blows across the Celetna road, along to the blackened sides of the Powder Tower after dark.

It is across this landscape that Lord Gustav preyed. Devils of the state conspired to deliver this nation from the inside to our enemies, and it was not to be tolerated. The worst of these complicit dogs were in the Interior Ministry. Our weak President Hacha, instead of being to blame, may be the only one holding these forces away from us. The university fascists and the sympathisers both in the west and here in Prague had already drawn up plans for the new occupation.

Gustav was not having it. With his handler and his interrogative skill, he identified all those at his show who he marked as traitors: workers at the ministry. One by one they were visited. A tap on the window before dawn. An encounter on a quiet hill. A deadly rendezvous in the park after nightfall.

Gustav is clever and shrewd. He hides the traitors away. Winding sheets and shallow pits dot the lonely woods of Chuchle, and soon grass will grow and we will lose their traces. The sewers contain more than dishwater and animal fats, and abandoned basements in the Old Town have been used once again after dark, for grim storage.

He is equal in his methods with both male and female enemies. After one show in the cold of January they found a sad-faced lady hanging in her own kitchen. Only stray dogs may have seen anything that night, a man hurrying away with an ornately clasped black case. The official judgment was suicide. Everyone agreed she never smiled.

And so it shall go, until we find freedom from threat.

"Karin," I slurred.

"Your pardon?"

"The lady was Karin."

Vaclav stroked his beard, and those lively grey eyes scanned mine. "You know of her?"

"She...my work." My mind fumbled the pieces of the night together, like a novice sculpting clay. My office had seemed so empty these past weeks, but my supervisor and I had thought that colleagues were just fleeing the approaching conflict.

"You work at the Interior Ministry?" asked Vaclav, his gaze fixed on me.

"Yes."

"Well, I see. I think that perhaps we need to have brandy." He stood up and, as he did so, his head entered the smoky shadows. He walked towards the far end of the bar with soft steps.

I sat up and swayed on my stool. This bar was open late. The figures on the perimeter maintained their huddled conversations and my eyes fell across the decanted liquor, the rows of thick beer glasses, and to the floor behind the bar where there sat a large black case, clasped ornately with silver buckles.

Vaclav returned. "The brandy is empty on the shelf. Stay here, I'll fetch the good one from the back room." He clasped his hand down on mine, and his rough skin felt like sandpaper.

I waited for him to disappear beyond view and then hurried out, clattering into a table on the way. The freezing night air rushed into my lungs as I hurried along the cobblestones and out to...who knew where? Marie had talked to me about my drinking and lack of presence of mind. I had no idea where I was.

Two hours later, I still don't.

I have tried to maintain a straight line, but each lane is darker than the last. The night air has worked some wine out of my head. A rising terror is clearing the fuzziness.

Branches knock in the trees like wooden shoes. Each clack of a shutter sounds like a linden cane on cobbles. Every gust of a leaf in the gutter reminds me of a string softly pulled.

And there, ahead in this narrow alleyway.

The smallest of figures.

The Undertow

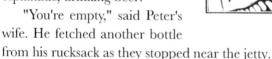

The first day of July brought delighted holidaymakers to Westbury Beach, but for Peter and Liz it was a day of sadness. They walked, like every other year, arm in arm along the esplanade, drinking beer.

"You're empty," said Peter's wife. He fetched another bottle from his rucksack as they stopped near the jetty.

"Here we are," he said, a breeze toying with his grey hair. They dropped to sit on the side of the concrete path, feet resting on the warm sand.

"To Kevin." Liz clinked her bottle with his. It was the fifteenth time they had toasted here. They put their heads together and hummed an old pop song, Kevin's favourite.

They sat in silence afterwards. Beyond, the high tide had brought in driftwood, seaweed, and a white rock. It moved oddly with the lapping of each small wave, as if it were lighter than stone. Curiosity got the better of Liz. She stood, then made a path around the sunbathers to fetch it.

"It's a conch," said Peter, turning the shell over. A deep red pattern curved away inside. "They can work as horns. You might get a note out of it if you try."

The shell tip was missing, which seemed an appropriate blow hole. Liz cleaned it with a splash of beer, then blew. A rasp rattled to the end of her breath, just spittle and air.

Peter tried, despite being fuzzy with drink. A brief parp followed a wheeze, so he persisted. Eventually a low sonorous note sounded out across the sand and waves, ancient and powerful.

And everything changed.

Peter was underwater, yet still sat on the esplanade. The salty sea, which his eyeballs had not touched since his fishing days, exploded around his face.

Instinctively, he grabbed his breath and looked over to Liz in terror. She was frozen in place, looking at him, no trace of discomfort on her face. The esplanade was visible for several yards before being lost in a briny murk.

Peter looked up as his lungs held. He had enough breath for a minute. He couldn't see the air above where he expected it to be but, in front of him where the shore had been, he saw the shimmer of a vertical surface with light beyond.

He pushed off and swam.

Just as his lung capacity ended, he broke through the wall of water and dropped onto sand.

He sucked in a big gulp of air, then looked back. A monolithic wall of churning water stood where the surf's edge had been. Beyond it, frozen beachgoers were locked in position; suspended whilst playing or sunbathing.

On Peter's side of the rift, where once there had been sea, land now stretched for miles. The coastal shelf had been replaced with a view from a descending plateau. A clear path stretched away and down.

Peter shook his ale-muffled head and tried to rationalise the situation.

He couldn't, so he started walking.

Peter hadn't travelled beyond the shore since the day Kevin drowned. He hadn't so much as taken a boat out anywhere. The idea of his son being at one with the brine all around him had been too much to bear.

He walked past objects as the path continued on. A few bits of material, boxes, some bottles. The trail dropped lower. Before long, a seal floated down from the sky.

"Excuse me," said the seal.

Peter stopped. This was strangely comforting as it pointed to a trip or dream.

"You shouldn't be here," said the seal.

"Yes, I know," replied Peter. "I am, though."

"Yes, so you are." The seal studied him for a moment, then twisted in a swimming motion, circling and examining him from every angle. "Oh," it said eventually.

"Oh?"

"Keep going, that way." The seal extended a flipper at five degrees to the path.

"Thank you. Before I go, where am I?"

"The Undertow. It will be open for you only for an hour. Leave everything here." With that, the seal swam back up into the air.

∾

Peter walked on, at five degrees to the path. He passed an anchor, some smashed wood, and tyres. He saw schools of flying fish, who pinged and chirped at him as they darted past. He passed crabs, surly crustaceans, who tutted and clacked their claws irritably at him. He walked past muttering flatfish and great, fat-lipped sea trout who implored him to turn back.

Looking to shore, he saw the great wall of water was just a remote barrier on the horizon.

Then he heard it. That pop song.

And there, by a rock, was his son, singing as sweetly as Peter remembered, still ten years old.

"Kevin!"

Kevin looked up, startled.

"Dad!" He rushed over and they embraced. Peter held him and they both wept.

"Come on," said Peter. Kevin nodded and took his hand, and they ran back up the path.

They laughed and chatted as they ran. Peter looked as much at his boy as the ground on which they rushed, his eyes drinking in that which he had thought lost.

As the hour approached, they neared the mighty wall of water. Peter could see that the very top of it was collapsing. The path around his ankles grew damp as the sea prepared to return.

Peter scooped Kevin up and ran. His son laughed and wrapped his arms around his father's neck. They reached the water wall just as it caved in.

∾

Peter staggered up the beach and dropped to his knees in front of Liz. With the closure of the Undertow, she sprang into motion.

The other beachgoers all moved too and soon turned to stare at the sound of Liz's screams.

Peter looked down.

His tears wetted those small white bones, which had long been picked clean by the gentle mouths of fish.

The Committee of Diligence

The Committee of Diligence
arrived at the library at 9am,
only to find it didn't open until
10 o'clock. Annoyed, they
whiled away an hour in their
cars, glaring at skateboarding
kids braving the summer heat.
The kids glared back.

Florence arrived, as she had
done for the last twenty years, at 9:50 precisely. The
Committee showed her the order. She read it carefully,
then invited them in. They pinned the document to the
library door, which they locked behind them.

Once inside, Florence offered them tea, as they
regarded the old and large library. The ruddy-cheeked
Officer Grady accepted it gladly, but Officers Hamer and
Fenton did not. Hamer swept along the aisles with her officials and Fenton bounded up the stairs to search the first
floor with his.

"I know this is inconvenient," said Officer Grady,

accepting a digestive biscuit, "but we can't be too careful. There could be dangerous, erm, things here." He waved the biscuit in the general direction of books. Florence quietly noted where the crumbs dropped.

"Should I leave?" she asked.

Grady thought not, but he went to see Officer Hamer to check.

Puffing back, he advised Florence that her knowledge of the place would be useful, and so she pottered about and caught up with some filing. Later she phoned the other librarians and told them to stay at home for the week.

Eventually large stacks of books and periodicals formed on the trolleys. Bakunin's *God and The State*, Klein's *No Logo*, and all the Chomsky titles joined Huemer, Rockwell, Rocker and Zinn. They also tossed in children's books: *The Red Balloon* ("subversive"), *The Lorax* ("clearly anti-capital"), and *Curious George* ("monkey") stacked up alongside Maurice Sendak's *Where The Wild Things Are*, which Officer Fenton described as "practically an anarchist guidebook".

Florence patiently went about her filing. Grady gave her an apologetic shrug every so often.

On Tuesday they informed Florence that, because of the size of the collection, the Committee planned to stay at the library all week, and perhaps into the next. Florence nodded and continued sorting index cards.

Later she checked if they had everything they needed, then retreated to her office for a break.

Inside, she lit a scented candle, slipped off her shoes and sat in her chair. Her arms relaxed on the armrests and she breathed deeply. Slowly, as she had practiced at least once a day for much of her adult life, she faded away from the day in meditation. The sound of tumbling books grew fainter for a while.

She imagined travelling up, rising above the loud city and the anger of the countryside. In her mind's eye she soared, away from the ports and borders and the shouting guards, and breached the atmosphere. She toured the stars. Her heart was light and receptive to the universe, and she smiled with happiness.

The universe saw Florence and smiled back.

The next day Officer Hamer approached Florence's desk.

"We've found the worst books," said Hamer, her pinched face pale under square-lensed glasses, "but we need your help to be certain."

Florence said she would be pleased to help.

Various sizeable galleries snaked off from the central hub. Florence suggested that, to save the Committee some time, they might like to split up and examine each corridor and gallery individually. Officer Fenton curtly agreed, annoyed that he hadn't thought of it himself.

Florence showed them each individual space and sub-chamber, positioning Officer Grady's team nearest the drinks stations, and so the Committee spread themselves out for the rest of the day.

On Thursday the travails resumed and Florence pottered here and there. Occasionally the sound of books slamming rose into the air, but this grew less frequent as the day went on. In the final three hours they tossed no books.

Florence looked up at the gallery balconies with a small smile.

Friday arrived. Hamer stalked up to Florence's desk. "Can you check, please? It's quiet. I just need to know everyone has a shelf to look at," she said brusquely.

Florence took a tour of the galleries. There the officials were. A few were talking to each other. Some were sitting cross-legged, absorbed in a book. One particular pair had met at a balcony and were passionately discussing something. One woman was holding a novel, Hesse's *Siddhartha*.

Florence baked an apple cake at the weekend. She dropped by to see her colleague Amie and reassured her that the library would be open soon. Amie worried about her job. Florence said it was going to be okay. They ate cake and watched trashy TV.

Monday came and the Committee gained access as usual, but there was a different atmosphere. Throughout the library debate arose in various aisles. At first Officers Fenton and Hamer told their officials off for talking too much, but Grady intervened and told them he had been chatting to some workers in the third gallery and it had been very interesting.

Tuesday, not a single book was thrown. The Committee ordered in pizza and Florence gave them all napkins for the crumbs. In the afternoon nearly all the officials had congregated in the grand forum in the centre of the building and talked for hours. And so it continued all week.

On Friday they abruptly left.

The books sitting on trolleys for removal remained uncollected. Florence called up Amie and together they started to re-shelve them.

Time passed. The nation went about its business.

Later that year the news broke that the government had sanctioned several officials in the Committee of Diligence on charges of subversion, and they had placed Officers Fenton and Hamer on administrative leave. Officer Grady could not be located at first but emerged much later as the leader of a new political party. The government weighed up the creation of a new department to take over their affairs and began preliminary interviews.

The city library remained ordered and tidy.

In the galleries the books rested silently on the shelves, with spines as strong as backbones.

The Aldwych Elevator

Amy smiled, but I just felt stupid. I looked at the feeble camera in my gloved hand and fumbled it back into my pocket. She adjusted her gleaming Go-Pro helmet-cam that had made mine look so inadequate and opened the old tunnel gate.

"Ready for the guided tour?"

"Yes," I lied. We walked into the dark, musty corridor beyond the prohibited sign, and away from the speeding cars.

Before long the sound of the London traffic grew faint.

"The UrbEx crew don't come here much, most head out to Russia," Amy called over her shoulder. The white of her skater helmet bobbed in the gloom ahead. "Loads of stuff over there; mines, sanatoria, military. Once they get abandoned, no one gives a shit about security."

"In Soviet Russia, places explore you?" I said with a woeful mock accent.

"Ha. Something like that. Here, take a shot of this for your uni project?" Her torch beam swung to the wall.

I took my camera out and shot a bank of dusty levers marked AUX. LINE EMERGENCY, which leaned under the roundel of the London Underground.

"So how far does this level stretch?" I asked.

"A mile or so. Mike's here somewhere, he came down just ahead of us with his guy."

~

Mike.

I knew I had no chance with Amy as soon as he'd appeared at the pub and given her a confident hug. Muscular and bearded, his tribal arm tattoos told a thousand alpha tales, even before I discovered he was so bloody nice as well.

The pub was a known Urban Exploration haunt, and there was another guy looking for a paid guide that night, so Mike had agreed to help him. I had sunk a few drinks and been so taken with chatting to Amy that I recall little about him, just pale smiling blue eyes as they agreed the deal. Because of the other man's schedule, Mike had agreed to take him down a couple of hours ahead of us.

~

Amy stopped by a fuse box, welded onto a wall by an elevator call button. "We're not interested in going far along, though. We're going down." She snapped a few switches in the box, then hit the button.

"This still works?"

"Yep, old freight elevator. It hooks the circuit up to the Piccadilly Line. Guess they never thought of disconnecting it. Don't worry, we can walk if it gets cut, it's just longer. You ok with this?"

I wondered how my anxiety could be so luminous in the gloom. "Yes, sure. If I get the pics and grade I want, then I'm happy."

Amy hummed a tune as we entered, then slammed the steel scissor gate shut behind us.

The elevator was lit with a single dim bulb. It had aluminium sides and was broad enough to carry several pallets down to the line when in use. Old childhood claustrophobia still gripped at my windpipe. The walls were marked, black dusty trails littering the surfaces. As we rumbled downwards, lights in a panel indicated the level.

Amy stretched a little and smiled. "Having fun?"

"Totally. Thanks again for this."

"No worries. Aldwych is the deepest of the disused stations. You'll get some great shots."

The lift juddered and Amy glanced up. "Just the cable playing out, it doesn't get used much. There's probably a nest up there."

The reassurance lasted seconds as something thudded onto the elevator roof.

"The fuck?" Amy stepped back and stared at the ceiling hatch.

"If that's a nest, I don't want to meet the rat, bird, whatever."

The elevator jolted to a stop. I looked at the scissor gate. Through its lattice was the smooth concrete of the shaft wall. We were in between floors.

"Christ," said Amy. "Give me a boost."

I propelled her up to the hatch, then she slid it across with a few whacks of her palm. As it grated open, something bulky dropped through.

"What the hell is that?" I couldn't quite discern the black shape in the light.

Amy landed back on the floor. The elevator shuddered as if trembling on the verge of restarting, and the bulb dimmed further. Somewhere above, power strained against power.

"What is it?" I said, staring at the inert blob on the floor.

Amy crouched and flicked on her halogen torch. It was a grey fabric rucksack, a red 'Anarchy' badge clear across its back. "It's...it's Mike's."

The lift shook and dropped a fraction. From above, a wet grinding sound echoed down the shaft.

Amy shone her light through the hatch, illuminating the old iron machinery above.

A figure writhed and jerked against the cogs. It was a man, hanging upside down, one leg thrashing about, the other flayed and bent backwards, grating in the straining steel cables surrounding the motor.

"Mike!" Amy screamed. The torch caught a flash of feral terror in his eyes.

He fell.

We had only moments to recoil aside as he plummeted onto the hatch. The elevator light blew out. Amy's torch slipped from her grasp and it rolled across the floor, the beam slashing the darkness.

The elevator, now freed, convulsed onwards down the

shaft. We were left in an inky blackness in which a gurgled, sucking sound rose from above.

My heart thumped against my chest as Amy scrambled for the torch and swung the beam upwards with a gasp.

Mike's torso and arms hung upside down through the hatch, suspended like a ghastly tapestry. One side of his head was matted and caved, like the collapsed shell of a hard boiled egg. The sucking sound escaping from his windpipe burbled into a splutter as bubbles of blood formed on his lips.

Amy gasped and leapt towards him, holding his chest. I was too numb to move and stared as she comforted his last breaths. His lips, shiny with blood, moved by her ear. After a while she pulled back and guided the torch back up through the hatch, between sobs. The light lanced upwards but met only the impassive blackness of the shaft.

"What...what is it?" My words half-caught in my throat.

"Devil," said Amy. "He said *Devil*."

～

Down.

Down.

It still travels.

I've tried to recall that night in the pub, searching for clues on what had arrived before us at the tunnels. The quiet and happy man Mike had spoken to. His neat attire and calm, kind blue eyes. I couldn't describe his face any further than that, it's just a blank.

The control panel doesn't respond. The floor indicator has now clicked round twenty times or more. We are far below the Piccadilly Line and dropping way beyond the deepest possible level.

The walls of the shaft have opened out to a dark

expanse. The lift descends by its thin cable ever lower, infinite and relentless. Amy sits mute with shock, rocking and wordless. This is beyond her experience and both our understanding. Mike, a lifeless butchery marionette, swings slaughtered and floppy above us. The floor is slick with blood. I feel it against my skin through my jeans.

The sheer terror grips at my stomach like a clamp. We are approaching a blazing lake of fire below; I can see it through the cage door slats. It is immense and blinding. The heat is towering.

Through stinging eyes I trace the blackened lines on the walls of the elevator.

Scorch marks, running like tears.

The Ravens of Villers-Bretonneux

Corporal Shaddick pivoted around, eyes probing the horizon.

A moment had passed between the terror of the Panzerwagen A7Vs roaring through the hedges at the far field edge and this uncanny, morbid calm. Silence now replaced the grating roar of the machines and the scrape of tracks clenching at the furrows. They'd crept like fingers of frost towards the ANZAC soldiers, heavy machine guns rattling in their casements. A foul, sweet stench of gasoline lingered in the air.

Perhaps he had lost consciousness. Where were the bodies?

He looked down at his pack, caked in the loam of Villers-Bretonneux, and hoisted it onto his back. He gripped his battered Enfield rifle and drew in a deep breath. A croak pulled his attention to a nearby tree. A raven gazed down with coal-chip eyes. Shaddick considered this for a moment. Birds had been absent for weeks, a mass migration leaving humans to their idiot carnage.

Beyond the tree line, the slope of a railway cutting dipped away. Low ground. Safety.

He stumbled towards the cutting, scanning the trees as he went. Where were Billy, Macca, and the other ANZACs? He must have blacked out. They wouldn't have left him, not his Aussie mates. Not in France.

The cutting continued for a few hundred yards, soaking grass lining the shrapnel dusted tracks, before arriving at a brick tunnel. Shaddick peered into the gloom, then checked back around. The air was deafening in its silence. He had no way of knowing where the battle lines had shifted to, so this passage could be the best way back to the west parish.

He stepped inside.

The pale light of day receded as he walked on. Fumbling in his pack, he pulled out his trench lighter and an electric TarnKapp torch. A couple of thumps with the edge of his hand struck up a dull, jaundiced glow.

Ahead, Shaddick saw only darkness, so concluded the route must curve. In the rush of the initial advance, he'd noticed neither rail line nor tunnel, and cursed himself for not paying more attention to the unit scout's monotonous briefing yesterday.

His footsteps crunched on the gravel between the sleepers, and a slow rhythm struck up as he advanced. The torch light projected ten feet forward at most, and to his left and right it just about picked out the damp stone tunnel walls.

His thoughts turned to Marie, and her smiling, tear-streaked face as she waved him off at Circular Quay three months before. When 1918 was still young. That bump beneath her summer dress.

Shaddick wondered if his daughter looked like him. Marie had written as much in her last letter. She implored him to stay alive, to keep his head on his shoulders. To come back to her, and to meet Helen.

Some chance in this farmland grinder.

Helen.

The name rode on his every breath.

Shaddick walked on.

The moment of the attack.

Billy, Macca, and Jevons had been with him, crouched ready on the eastern flank of the field. Jevons was nervous, but Billy was his usual jocular self.

"Look, Jevs, I'm not sure you're bloody cut out for this. Don't piss yourself."

"For Christ's sake Bill, shut it."

"Don't bring Christ into this. Think of a pair of French legs, that'll see you through. God left this shitty fucking country last year, he ain't coming back, mate."

They had known about the German motorised position for a week, but it was their shit luck it would start moving just as they were about to attack. Major Holmlee wanted to catch the enemy unawares, seeing as the main front was four miles to the south.

Senseless plan, as usual.

Gunfire cracked through the air as soon as they set foot in the field. They all hit the soil straight away. On the north edge Brannigan's platoon caught the worst of it. Shaddick witnessed Brannigan himself convulse as bullets volleyed through the captain's body like a swarm of lead hornets.

And then the tanks. Those bloody tanks.

Of course, the allies fielded their own Mk. IVs. When not being repaired, these crept blindly ahead of the infantry, like rattling idiot gods. Better than machines at the back - more than one ANZAC brave had been clipped by their own tank's tracks, rolling over a forward position.

The German tanks were different. Slab sided and brick-shaped, the standard rifles did nothing to the plate. Devil help the unit without armour-piercing rounds that ran up against them.

Shaddick's platoon carried no AP that morning. Just peas in pea shooters.

That gasoline smell. Hades must have the same odour.

This tunnel. So long.

After a time, visibility lightened. It was peculiar, as daylight was still absent at the far end. Perhaps the torch was catching a different rock type. Luminous moss, possibly. A faint sound reached Shaddick from overhead, beyond the roof. The tunnel should be on the downside of the hill by now.

Perhaps it was a trick of the gloom, but the tunnel walls were deep red, the colour of Marie's lipstick the day he'd met her.

That night they danced and laughed at Scotty's club near to King Street Wharf, rain pelting down as they ran to the cab. The next November they married in a chapel in the hills, kissing in front of the world like the only humans on earth.

Seven months later, Ferdinand lay dead in Sarajevo.

The world marched into the chasm.

Now the tunnel walls beside him looked yellower, reminding Shaddick of the canola and mustard crops on his dad's farm. Those 6am starts helping with the harvest and the rattling, ancient cart carrying the crop to the barn. The saltbox farmhouse and his mother standing by the horses, a brush in one hand, stroking along a mane with the other. Her red hair alight in the sunshine like fire. The New South Wales sky and the 'oo-wa' call of the pied currawongs in the old trees lining the farmyard.

The sound through the roof of the tunnel was getting louder, a kind of clattering. Shaddick paused and took a step towards one wall. It faded as he did so, and he saw that there was no tunnel side, just a dim, ambient light. He scrambled back, and with shock couldn't locate the tracks. The ground all around was solely gravel.

A small knot of panic clenched Shaddick's windpipe as disorientation set in.

Where was he?

He stopped and blinked. The yellow glow around him changed to blue. Again, memories forced their way into his mind.

Blue skies. He had lain on his back on warm days and watched the clouds make the shapes of magical beasts. Their impassive eyes watched him from miles overhead, and only mercy or indifference prevented them from leaning down and devouring him in one bite. Blue like the sea at Coogee Beach in the summer, Thompson's Bay from Dolphin's Point, that sunken cobalt depth. The foam had spiked on the waves and the water seemed like the space between the stars some evenings.

Shaddick ran forward, away from these memories, holding the feeble torch in front like a shield. He needed to be out of this wretched place and headed back to Australia the first moment he could. His past recollections were joining up like magnets and pulling him, compelling him to return home. He was a new father for Christ's sake - this wasn't his bloody war.

He fled in the direction he had been walking but the ground sloped downwards, tipping his gait back on his heels.

The clattering grew louder.

The surrounding light shifted to grey, like the clouds of gas he had seen shell adjacent hills. His unit had passed a gas attack area just a week before. The corpses of men and horses were stiff and rictus-arched by the roadside, akimbo in gullies, prone and ghastly across paths.

This ground was getting too steep. Shaddick stopped and backtracked but this too led downhill. Every direction was downhill! The ground had fallen away at each point around him. The gravel filtered away as he stood stationary, like shingle being sucked from underfoot by the receding wash of a wave.

The sound from above swelled. Tears stung his eyes. He was going to fall. Only a child could balance on a patch of ground so small!

A child.

Helen! Hold on! He was coming home!

That sound; growing, clattering and cawing.

Ravens, thousands of ravens.

In the bloody muck of the field at Villers-Bretonneux, Billy closed Shaddick's lifeless eyes and looked up at the black birds that had taken flight so noisily. They must have heard something, perhaps the crack of a distant shot.

Jevons looked down at Shaddick. "Say anything?"

"No mate, just bled out, nothing there."

They waited, grim and silent, as allied battlefield carts approached from the western camp.

The King of Gorse

I was trying to help. Now I might never sleep properly again.

I'd spoken to Kay twice. You build bridges where you can in rural Dorset. We hadn't swapped more than pleas- antries, but I gained the impres- sion of a conflicted character  beneath her dreadlocks and earth-mother tattoos. She lived with her daughter in a pretty, ivy-clad studio which nestled by the side of the main lane, between my cottage and the post office. We were at the north end of the village, and beyond our cottages the road snaked away uphill, enclosed by dark, gorse-lined heathland. During the week Kay worked in the gallery in the village centre, selling her beau- tiful stencil work, but that morning she was smoking in her garden; with teeth clenched, shivering.

"Morning. Everything ok?" I called through my open

kitchen window. She looked for a second, then beckoned me over.

She wasn't the small talk type and got to the point. It transpired that Rose, her four-year-old daughter, had come into her bedroom that morning, caked in mud and unable to say a word. "Can you come and check her over, Doctor Hall?" she asked.

I had retired from surgery practice three years before, and would have been delighted not to see another cough, sniffle or headache till I reached the grave, but — bridges and all that.

She showed me in.

Rose was sitting in the colourful lounge, watching a wacky cartoon on a little TV, expressionless. The patio doors were open. Beyond, a man in a green top sat on the grass in the sunny back garden. Kay took me to one side.

"The front door was open." she said.

"This morning?"

"Yes." She wiped her brow, remorse etched on her face. "Her dad's back. It wasn't him though, he was in bed all night. He sleeps like the dead."

I crouched by Rose. They had cleaned her up, but I checked her face and body over her clothes and could only see some minor scratches about her knees.

"Rose," I said, the old calm manner deployed, "I'm Doctor Hall. You remember me, I live across the lane?"

She nodded.

"Do you remember what happened last night?"

She paused, then shook her head.

I returned to Kay. "She has some abrasions, but with kids it's hard to tell where they pick up those things."

Kay looked at the floor, her eyes restless. "Doctor Hall, there's another thing. We left some...mushrooms by the door in the hall last night. The pack was on the floor this morning, lighter than we left it...I think."

I struggled to hide my disapproval.

"You think she had some? Was she sick at all?"

Her jaw tightened. She shook her head but looked lost.

"Would you give me permission to try light hypnosis? We should be able to get an account of the night."

I fetched my voice recorder from the house. We started when I returned and she went under easily.

I've transcribed the session here, just as she spoke that morning.

26/08/12 10:15am - Account of Rose Walker (aged four) regarding overnight period on 25th August 2012.
Clinician: Dr EL Hall (ret'd).

(Initial trance inducement - 40 seconds)

ELH: Rose, can you tell me what happened last night?

RW: I was awake. I wanted a drink. It was hot, and I needed one. I went to the kitchen and used the water tap on the fridge. I use the ice cube thing when Mum lets me, but it's loud so I didn't.

ELH: Did you eat anything, Rose?

RW: Yes, banana and sweets.

ELH: Where were they?

RW: The banana was on the kitchen top and the sweets were in the hall by the door.

ELH: How many sweets did you have?

RW: Just one, but it tasted bad, like dirt.

ELH: What happened then?

RW: Went back to bed.

ELH: Did you go to sleep?

RW: No, I felt a bit spinny. I shut my eyes, but didn't sleep as it got light.

ELH: Daylight?

RW: No, just light. Bright. I didn't want to wake Mummy; she had stopped crying and was asleep.

(At this point Kay Walker interrupts, but I ask her to wait until the end of the session. She agrees.)

ELH: What did you do?

RW: Went to play.

ELH: Outside?

RW: Yes. It was bright.

ELH: Tell me what happened when you went to play.

RW: I opened the door and went to the garden, but there was music and it was bright. The sky wasn't bright; the ground was bright, and the air was low down, sort of. The hedges in the garden were funny and wriggly. The music came from along the road and some banging and stuff. The garden was empty and my bike was in the shed, so I went to the road and went to see where the music was.

ELH: How far did you go, Rose?

RW: There were no cars, so I walked and the trees were wriggly. I saw rabbits and worms and a fox. They were talking, but the worms weren't talking, they were hissing like cats sometimes hiss. The ground was like glass and I saw Mrs Calloway, the old lady Mum doesn't like, and she pointed up the road so I went that way. She was smiling.

(Kay Walker again interjects. She shouts upstairs and leaves the house. The session continues as Rose is in a good trance and lucid.)

RW: I left at the path where Dad used to walk Brucie when he was alive and went along the path and saw some eggs under a tree and some bundles of sticks and a horse.

The horse looked backwards and funny. There was a light in the sky and it was floating over the tree at the end of the path but then it went but the ground was still bright. In the grass by the path were some people and they had faces like birds but some had faces a bit like, sort of fish? They were dawdling and turning, and each time one turned, the other one turned. It looked silly. The end of the path was bright, but after that it was dark. Old Mrs Calloway pointed again, and she was pointing towards the end of the path, so I went there. She seemed smiley, but her arms were shiny-fuzzy. I wasn't cold at all.

ELH: What happened then?

RW: I went to the end of the path and the ground stopped being bright and was a sort of blue. But it was a dark blue. I was near the trees there and the start of the hill that Brucie used to run up when he knew there was a stick Dad would throw. The field next to it was dark and I could hear a sort of monster in that field or something, which sounded like a lot of bees...but the bees could speak, but I didn't understand the words. I didn't want to go into that field but Mrs Calloway pointed up the hill instead so that was good. I said phew! The gorse bushes go up the hill and sometimes they have flowers but are spiky, so I know not to touch those.

ELH: You walked all the way up the hill?

RW: Yes. Mrs Calloway was next to me at the bottom and she said there was a king at the top and he would like to see me and make me a princess if I was good. I walked up the hill, it's not far, I've been up it lots. As I went up, I could see stones and some holes in the ground, like rabbits live in, but they weren't for rabbits. The bushes at the top looked like a chair and there was a man in the chair and he was smiling. I didn't think he looked like a king, but he said he was one.

ELH: What else happened?

RW: He said he was very old and made from the gorse bushes. He moved really slowly. He asked if he had permission to come to the village and be the king there as well. He said it was important that I said yes and he would not come if I didn't want him to.

ELH: Is that all you remember?

RW: We made friends, so I came back with him.

ELH: Where did he go to?

RW: Into the back garden. He's there now.

26/08/12 10:50am - Session halted.

Rose curled up on the sofa and looked at the TV, and I don't think she noticed my shock. I went to the patio doors and looked out into the garden. The wooden gate was open. The man was no longer there.

Returning to the hallway, Kay was nowhere to be seen. She was annoyed during the session at the mention of Mrs Calloway, muttering something like "that woman", and had sworn up the stairs before slamming the front door. A shaven-haired man in a white vest looked blearily over the banister. It was Rose's dad, an occasional dweller in the house, just rising.

He came downstairs and we had a quick introduction. He didn't seem phased at the commotion Kay had caused and traipsed into the kitchen as I left.

I returned to my cottage and made some tea before settling into the upstairs study for some reading. The study had a large panoramic window that took in the rolling downs and lane, so I'd be able to see when Kay returned. I mulled over the session with Rose.

She seemed physically fine, which was the key thing. If she had ingested any of the mushrooms, it didn't seem to have affected her adversely, and probably accounted for her tale of the night. In fact, she may well have not gone beyond the front garden at all if she'd been tripping. The imagery she'd described was vivid and powerful, but there were few forces more potent than a child's imagination, let alone one exposed to a mild narcotic.

Hours passed, and the warm morning evolved into a balmy afternoon. After lunch I walked down the short hill into the village.

As I strolled, I tried to recall exactly what Kay had said when she had left during the session. It was something about Mrs Calloway, who was an elderly lady living on the main lane close to the village green. I didn't really know her. From what I had gathered on my occasional forays into The Green Man inn, most of the villagers didn't seem to want to know her.

I drew close to Mrs Calloway's cottage. A fresh cigarette butt was on the grassy pavement and the oak front door was open. What looked like small pine needles were scattered on the garden path.

"Mrs Calloway?" I called at the door. With no answer, I ventured into the hall, and following a murmuring sound, entered her drawing room. The heavy curtains were half-drawn, and suddenly the bright August day seemed far away.

Mrs Calloway, small and thin with white hair and a red dress, sat at her table.

"Sun, moon, dandelion, gorse," she muttered, before looking up at me. Her eyes blazed. My mind seemed to lurch at her gaze, tipping forwards into an unsteady place.

"Ah, Mrs Calloway. Sorry to disturb you," I stammered.

Her expression was triumphant, and her eyes shone like green fire.

I continued. "Have...have you seen Kay Walker? I think she was coming to see you."

"Sun, moon, dandelion, gorse," she repeated, this time nearly a whisper. My head echoed with the words. I held on to the doorframe as my sense of balance tipped sideways slightly. Her mantra continued. "Sun, moon, dandelion, gorse. At last he is here!"

The air thrummed with unheard vibrations, and I felt a yearning to be clear of this cottage. Kay had been here, but no more. Mrs Calloway, her eyes ecstatic, rocked gently. Her tone became lower and more guttural, and she seemed like a small grey and green whirlpool in front of my eyes. I looked at her table and for the first time in the shaded gloom saw a scattering of sticks and a small, lifeless bird.

I hurried into the village centre.

There were plenty of folks about. They walked between the small row of shops, the war memorial, and the village green, but the road was empty of cars. Every so often I passed scattered clumps of those small plant needles. Rose sat on the green, with no adult nearby.

"Hello Rose."

"Hello Doctor Hall."

"What are you doing here, where's your mum?"

She swept her hands across the grass, the blades tickling her palms. "She's not coming back like she was, or Dad," she said, before looking along the road and pointing.

A tall man wandered from door to door, about a hundred yards away. He wore a green tunic, and it seemed to slide and convulse over his similarly green-hued skin. His hair was wild and unkempt, and his chin jutted like the prow of an old ship. He opened the door to Mr Peterson's house, walked in, and then emerged about a minute later. He then entered the Robinsons', then Mrs Bolton's cottage, then the hairdresser shop. He was methodically calling at each property and had no trouble gaining entrance. I couldn't quite make him out. His form seemed blurry and indistinct. As he exited the hairdressers, I saw some people standing inside motionless, and others lying prone.

"You should go," said Rose. "He's seeing who will follow. He'll open the field gate for anyone left. The things in there will come to town."

I went to pick Rose up but she wriggled away. Across the street, the green figure emerged and looked directly over to where we were. He shook his blurry head and opened his mouth abnormally wide, as needles fell to the floor.

"He knows about you Doctor Hall," said Rose. "He wants to see you too."

I backed away and fled up the lane as fast as I could.

I packed quickly, but before leaving I looked out across the village from my study window. A deep primal fear coursed through my veins. Through the village, something old stalked.

I've been at my sister's now for a week. She thinks I'm

under the weather and has been very kind in giving me space. What can I say? At night I sleep in small flurries, and my dreams are thick with the rustling of leaves and a sound like a thousand bees. My sister lives at the other end of the downs and in my mind's eye I can travel across the rolling hills to the outskirts of the village, but no further.

Something in me has been changed by his stare. The village is no longer under the dominion of people; I can tell from old whispers in my sleeping hours.

My dreams tell of the clicking of crickets and the creak of lonely ash and beech. The brush of wind across the bluebell meadows and the soft clawing of the badgers deep in their setts. Starlings know, wheeling high in packs in the summer air.

The King is back.

The Fourteenth Day

Elias traced his hand across the picture on the wall. It showed children running and laughing among trees in the sunshine. There was a girl on the far right-hand side, but the paint had peeled away, so she had no head. Elias thought she must have looked pretty. Perhaps she was also ten years old.

Outside the window a similar sun shone down, as it did every day on the outskirts of Damascus. Otherwise the sky was empty. Where rotor blades, vapour trails and glinting wings flew, just clear, perfect azure stretched into space.

Elias walked across to the window and huffed on it, drawing a circle with his finger. The other kids had often been bored, but not Elias. He liked the quiet times. He enjoyed the small sounds and seeing things the others missed when it was still. Right now he could quietly trace the curves in the rubble of the building opposite, the tattered sand-coloured walls and exposed pipes. Elias wondered where the people who lived there had gone.

The quiet of the morning revealed a few cars driving towards the hospital along the main street. Elias hadn't seen cars for days. The last ones he had seen were local people hastily loading up old trucks -- they must have packed all they owned! He had heard them shouting in the street below and then they had raced away, towards the hill. The cars approaching today came from the other direction. Armed men walked alongside them and a big gun was mounted on the leading car.

Elias was bored of guns. He turned back and looked around the nursery ward. The hospital had made the room as fun as could be. Soft toys lolled about in a big crate, and colourful chairs stood stacked next to chalk slates and a magnetic letter board. There were other, more random things. In the corner two shopping trolleys acted as stands for pictures, and the week Elias first arrived a big man had come in and left a large animal-skin rug in the middle of the room. The other kids had enjoyed rolling around on that before being taken home.

He turned back to the window. Voices rose as figures approached. It sounded like normal Arabic, but the faces of the men were all sorts. One even had a red beard, how funny. A tanker lorry drove up and Elias peered forward as far as the glass would allow. The lorry reversed to the hospital doors and the men scurried around it. One man with a long rifle looked up at the hospital from the other side of the street. He seemed to scan each window. He looked at Elias and for a few seconds they just stared at each other. The man lowered his eyes as if he was sad.

Elias thought maybe they were looking for the injured soldiers who had come in last week. Doctor Burhan had come into the nursery and told him not to worry about the noisy men on trolleys in the corridor, just that they needed some help and Doctor Burhan was going to give it to them. He helped everyone. Elias believed he was the kindest doctor in the world.

The men in the street were feeding out some hoses from the tanker to the front door. How odd. The driver got out and threw a lever, then all the men stood back and waited.

Elias went back to the center of the room, lay down on the rug and stared up at the ceiling. There were luminous stars up there, but he couldn't see them in the daytime.

A scream went up from beyond the door, perhaps from down the stairs. A metal crash rang out as if someone had knocked something over. Elias had heard lots of screams in the past few years. In fact, he couldn't remember a day without them. He'd never seen the point of shouting, especially at the planes. They couldn't hear you up there. He wondered if pilots ever screamed, then thought perhaps they did when they got worried.

Elias raised his legs and looked at his feet. It would be nice to walk somewhere different someday, maybe when he was better. Perhaps when Mother and Father get back -- they had been gone for fourteen days. He asked Doctor Burhan when they would come back. He always replied "in time," and then wanted to talk about something else.

More crashing and noise.

Elias picked up the sound of an engine running. He looked over at the wall painting and noticed something strange but pretty. A tendril of mist curled out of the vent and glided across the ceiling. It was a faint yellow, like the flowers he'd seen in books. Behind it, more puffed from the grille and swirled above his eyes.

A faint bang from downstairs, like the pop of a cork. Some shouting.

The yellow haze dropped slowly lower. Elias would see what it smelled like soon.

The door opened, making him jump a little. It was Doctor Burhan. He was crawling on all fours like a cat.

"Elias, come, like this!" he said, and they both scrambled out of the room.

Doctor Burhan seemed worried about the noises from downstairs. He carried Elias up and up so many flights of stairs. The soft bump of his steps reminded Elias of when Father used to carry him before the town was different, before people stayed indoors when planes came.

A tremendous crash came from below.

As Doctor Burhan opened the door to the roof and the sun blazed down, Elias remembered riding on Father's back in the dawn's brightness, and how white birds used to fly in great flocks in the clear blue sky.

Twenty Steps to the Ditch

Cal said drink'd be the death of me. I hate it when that bastard's right. He'll mourn, like the rest, but that bloody smugness will endure for longer.

Cal drank the same amount as me every Friday at the Forty Crowns; eight or nine pints of malty ale passing under his moustache, but he never seemed to lose his air of sage sobriety. Perhaps it was his sixteen stone against my ten. Either way, I'd get shitfaced; my little hobby at the end of a dull working week.

I had programmed my route home when the closing bell rang. Straight out of the car park to the lane, turn right, twenty steps to the old drainage ditch underneath streetlights that hadn't worked for years, then left across the viaduct. Straight ahead for a mile. The lamps then appeared again and my house soon after, heating on, key under the mat, and some carb-heavy ready meal primed for the microwave. I'd done it in power cuts, the fog and, last Christmas, through a blizzard. I reckon no matter how much he drinks, a real man can find his way home. Inner compass like a Swiss watch, me.

That Friday I said cheerio to Cal and Bess, bade Gayle the barmaid goodnight — "Marry me. Still no? Fair enough" — shook hands with June the landlady, announced "I'm leaving!" to a chorus of "bugger off then" and staggered out to the road. June had got some double-strength IPA in. As a result, I struggled to fix on the horizon through the rotating angles of the lane, the road-side hedges floating under the inky night sky.

I started counting steps as I veered into the gloom; one, two, three, bloody tasty pint, five, I've got to jack the job in, seven, I miss Sarah, ten. I wonder what she's doing now, twelve, still with that arsehole I bet, some swanky weekend away I bet, fifteen, well bollocks to them, thirteen.

Thirteen? I think. I took two more steps and my third footfall met only air.

After a heavy tumble, I slammed to a halt in the ditch and cackled; the beer anaesthetising any pain. Thank hell Cal hadn't seen that. He'd have pissed himself for weeks.

"You idiot," I said.

"Me?" replied a scratchy voice.

I turned to the right towards the words and saw two green lights. They blinked. "You can see me?" said the voice, like twigs scraping a window.

"Uh, yes." I squinted and tried to pick out my companion.

Silence lasted for way too long, then the moon peeked past the clouds above. A squat black figure sat in the ditch, eating something. It could have been a bit of a sheep, cat, or something far worse. Its needle teeth scraped the skin off bones and a barbed tongue, twice the length of its bulbous, ape-like head curled around the flesh, pulling it away in shearing slivers.

"We have a problem," it said, after finishing munching.

"I don't think so," I ventured in reply.

It looked at me from deep green watery sockets, as if weighing up a decision, before shifting and letting out a belch. "I'm full," it announced.

"That's good."

"Yes, I think it probably is. If I see you again, I will carve the skin from your back and eat you alive in small portions." It shifted to one side and, as it did so, a little bell tinkled around its neck. I glimpsed thick, powerful limbs, and something else, wriggling and trapped behind it.

I'm pretty confident after a few drinks, but I'm not too proud to admit my bladder failed.

"Ugh," said the thing. "Go."

I made a couple of pitiful attempts to haul myself out of the slippery trench before crawling onto the tarmac lane, caked in mud. A streetlight had blinked on, which helped me see. As I turned to look down, the thing in the ditch lowered its hand, the bell tinkled, and the streetlight went out again.

The clouds soon parted, and moonlight showed me the way across the viaduct to home.

I kept away from the Forty Crowns for a couple of weeks and drank at home instead. Not quite the same though, and all those bloody thoughts.

On the Thursday of the third week Bess popped into the office and told me to get my sorry arse to the pub tomorrow. It was a quiz night and my twin specialities of 'European motor sport' and 'Nazi history and armaments' would be in demand.

So I went, but we still lost. I drank a few and got a cab home. After that I resumed going on Fridays, but made a point of walking left through the village for an extra half mile instead of the shorter route over the viaduct.

Today's Saturday, maybe Sunday. This week's trip to the pub is coming back to me in little bursts.

It was Cal's birthday. Lots of drinks, Christ; Russian porter, that toffee-like best bitter from the local brewery, followed by a seasonal special June had brought in from Wales. We had scotch too and some evil brown chasers in small thick glasses that Bess bought. They tasted like paraffin, and I had three. Maybe four.

I was utterly smashed and forgot myself. I was chatting to Cal, who was walking back to my side of the village to see his new girlfriend. Out to the road, turning right, twenty steps to the ditch.

Two green fiery eyes glinted low down in the dark.

My terror rose as it clambered out, the bell tinkling. Its smile revealed hundreds of needle-sharp teeth behind dry, blackened lips as the lamps above blinked on and off. Cal shouted, "What? What's there?" as I stumbled backwards in wild panic. He couldn't see it, but he was looking right at it!

I scrambled away and clipped the lip of the viaduct, that crumbling gap where the wall met the road, and fell forty feet, straight down onto the railway line.

I heard the bleeping of a machine and smelled the sterile air long before I could open my eyes in the private ward. The doctor told me I'd been very lucky. I couldn't move a muscle, and tubes made it impossible to speak.

She explained I was at the city hospital and listed my injuries: two broken vertebrae, a shattered shinbone, a hairline crack through the hip, a torn quad, a dislocated pelvis, three broken ribs and a mashed-up collar bone. My right wrist had also snapped and I had a mild concussion. They're worried about organ damage and I have many sensors hooked up. Cal came and went; he said something or other, but the morphine makes me forgetful. He looked sorry. I think he said something about Sarah, but maybe I imagined that.

I wonder what she's up to, and whether she knows I'm here.

It's night now. I'm high on the twelfth floor and my body cast means I can only look to the left, out of the window. Twenty minutes ago I saw the streetlights blink out on the ring road leading to the hospital, then relight, one by one. The same thing happened all the way down the drive towards this building, before the last one blacked out, just under my line of sight above the window ledge, a few minutes ago.

There are hardly any nurses on duty at night after the recent cuts.

The TV reflects a series of dimming lights in the hallway. I can't turn to see.

The machine still bleeps, but a little bell tinkles too. Through the morphine I feel a firm, slicing pressure on my leg cast.

Drink will be the death of me.

Bloody Cal.

The Screes

CUMBRIA CONSTABULARY PENRITH
TRANSCRIPT OF AUDIO STATEMENT BY CLARE
FARISS 5/6/2009
RE: CASE 234/56B MISSING PERSONS (ELIZABETH
FARISS)

Ok. Some background. I travel
all the time with my work, but
try to see my sister as often as I
can. Liz had been getting better
and was writing to me again.
She just sounded lonely. I have
no idea if she is still on her
medication; she didn't say.

    I told her I was taking time
off so maybe we could go hiking, like the old days. She's
been in a poky little flat in Whitehaven near Dad's. She
hasn't really wanted to do much since her son Daryl ran
away a few years back. He was such a lovely bright boy and

must have left a terrible hole. Getting out on the fells always used to be fun, especially when she had her troubles in her teens. And besides, I've been trying to lose weight.

We packed some lunch, a map, a compass, lip balm for the chilly wind, and headed up onto the Wasdale trail, the one that runs above the screes. You must be careful on that path as on one side the loose slopes run straight down into Wastwater Lake.

We walked along, chatting a bit, although she's never that talkative at the best of times. She kept looking over the path edge, down the steep screes, to the water. We walked silently for a while. I guess I lost her in the beauty of it, and she me.

Then the mist came down. Cairns mark the path, so there was no need to head back. Fog comes and goes on the high fells, as I'm sure you know.

Liz froze. I don't know what she saw. I couldn't see anything. She grabbed my arm and shouted "look!" but it was just a foggy, rocky path.

She screamed, terrified, then ran off. I tried to go after her, but couldn't keep up. That was four days ago, and I haven't seen her since. I'm really worried.

Please find her.

Newcastle Church Housing Association
230 Galston Street
Newcastle Upon Tyne
NE1 8XS

2nd February 2014

Dear Clare,

I don't know if you are still at this address. I've not been in touch for so long, and I just needed to write to let you know that I have some sense at last. I've gotten hold of some pills and they seem to help. I keep on the move. I don't know when you'll see me again. I am being hunted.

The schizophrenia came back. It's been with me forever, I know. It's made me see the world as a terrible place, but I have a real confession to make before it is too late.

I have to tell you. Daryl didn't run away. I know what I told the police back then, but I couldn't tell them what I'd done. I couldn't tell them that my son often looked at me with the eyes of the Devil, or that I knew he was planning to poison me. They'd have locked me up again.

One night I woke up and could hear him whispering to me from the back room. The back room! Only the Devil could whisper that far. I rose and went in and he was there, asleep. His mouth and eyes were shut, but his whispering carried on. Threats, curses and foul language. Terrible words.

I did what I had to do. I put the pillow over his head and pushed. He was strong for a twelve-year-old, but I dropped all my weight onto him until he stopped thrashing about. I wept for an hour. No mother should have to do that to her child.

I wrapped him in his red coat, dragged him to the car and drove to Wastwater Lake. I loaded his pockets with rocks and pushed him into the water. I can still see his open Devil's eyes, glassy and accusing, as he drifted down into the depths.

The police investigation went cold, as you know. I wanted to walk up on the screes with you and try to make peace with what I had done. Guilt tormented me. I just wanted to say a prayer for my lost boy.

After the fog came down I saw what looked like a wet sack in the middle of the path, crumpled and red. As I froze, it uncurled itself and a figure stood to face us. I knew Daryl's coat. His skin was awful; grey and waxy, like a melted candle. He seemed to cry out but made no sound, then raised his arms and came towards me. The Devil was in his rotted eyes! If I had stayed, he would have murdered me on the spot.

I fled back to town, caught the first train and ended up in Leeds. I don't let folks know my actual name. I eat donations from the shelters I stay at. My nerves are bloody fried.

At night in sleep I see a red coat floating towards me, flapping in the wind. I know he's coming for me, so I keep moving.

Dear God, help me.

Yours,

Liz

Excerpt from *A Medium's Life* by Carlton Soane, published by HarperCollins (2016):

Of course, not all the spirits I commune with are adults. Some of the most heartbreaking séances that I have had are those involving visitations by children. They very rarely make sense.

I was staying in the English Lake District last summer, and during a hotel session I recorded a visitation by a teenage boy. Here is his message, word for word. I could not make head nor tail of it.

"It's cold here, and dark all the time. I can't remember how I got here. I can leave the water and go up the slope to the path at the top, but no further. I see people walk by sometimes, but they never look at me. It's so lonely."

Then, after a pause, he cries out joyfully.

"Mam! I'm here!"

In tribute to Ambrose Bierce (1842-1914)

Gently Rises the Grain

It had been a weird summer from the first hot day.

With Brexit looming and visas for staying in Britain becoming tricky, all the local farms had taken a hit. Glenn had been quite lucky; his only Polish worker, Pavel, had always intended to return home in June, so the planning was in place. Old McAllister's place on Crow Hill had seen three Romanians vanish overnight. They just upped sticks and left. Who could blame them?

Still, Glenn reasoned that McAllister could manage. He was a rich old arse.

Glenn lamented the guy's wealth in The Red Lion last Friday.

"Brand new bloody tractor," he slurred. "Two crop sprayers too. Undercutting bastard."

"Looks affer his outgoings, dunn'e," replied Jack Kendall, behind his bar. "Never comes swillin' in 'ere like you lot. Probably why 'e's got the coin."

"Well, someone's got to keep you in business."

Jack gave him that look of his, then ambled off to a remote part of the old inn.

Glenn then caught the eye of the man who would kill him.

He was minding his pint in the corner, slim-faced, and flat cap still on despite the heat. They kept each other's gaze long enough for one of them to have to say something, in that awkward English way.

"Good health," said Glenn.

The man tipped his glass slightly in reply.

The rest of the night became hazy as, yet again, Glenn drank beyond his limit.

He guessed he'd spoken further to the fellow. There he was in his flat cap the next day, at Glenn's door.

"Yes?" Glenn muttered blearily.

"I'm here, so." The man's eye was steady and his tone gruffer than his youthful years. Vague memories swam back.

"Did I...did we?"

"We spoke, I'm here about the arrangement."

"Erm." This wasn't the first time Glenn had lost track of an evening, although it was more common in his younger days, and usually it was some lass he had to recall offending. Still, folks were not left standing at the door in these parts.

In the man came and he soon had a cup of tea in front of him. Molly appeared, and smiled and pottered about collecting her car keys, then left for work.

"Your wife?"

"Yes. Look, what did...?"

"She's nice." He took a deep sup, despite the tea having been on the boil only a minute before.

"I'm sorry, you must forgive me..."

"Yep, you had a couple of drinks, but you meant what you said. In case you don't remember, I'm Lewis."

"Lewis, right."

"And we shook on it." Lewis's eyes were dull but steady.

It transpired that, as the evening had progressed, Glenn had ranted more and more about McAllister. Like many a drunk, his volume went up as the drinks went down, and before long most of the patrons had drifted away. He had harangued the door, the walls, his drink, and eventually Lewis. And Lewis had listened.

He had listened to Glenn's resentment, his stress, and had eventually revealed that he worked up on Crow Hill for the object of Glenn's ire. He serviced the machines, fixed the outbuildings and shot the vermin. And he had no love for old McAllister.

"Callous fucker, really," Lewis had said. "He used to clout them Romanian boys. They only got one meal a day."

The words came back to him and listening to Lewis's steady voice in the kitchen flicked his usual switches regarding Crow Hill.

"Anyway, I'll pick you up Friday," Lewis finished.

"I'm still not sure about..."

"Breaking into the barn. That's where he keeps the deeds."

With that he departed, leaving Glenn in no doubt he would be back on Friday.

~

"What deeds?" said Molly as they sat down to dinner that evening.

"I think it was about the north field," Glenn replied, chewing his omelette.

The top field had been a two-generation point of contention for their family and McAllister's. Glenn's grandpa, who had first set up the farm, always insisted that the field belonged inside the old feudal boundaries of their farm. They had left it fallow as Grandpa's health took a turn for the worst and, as he had not fenced or hedged the field, there was no one to prevent McAllister's father, Barney, from including it in his own boundary claim in 1950. By the time Glenn's father had returned from military service to take over the running of the place, the dispute was set in stone.

"The thing about Grandpa is he kept no papers," Glenn said. "In reclaiming that land, we had nothing to show."

A few whiskies by the fire convinced him that this was an opportunity. He would go with Lewis and see what came of it. That top field was enormous and perfectly suited to their stock. It could make a real difference to Glenn and Molly's future; they were just scraping by.

~

The rest of the week passed calmly. Molly was still her distant self. Things hadn't been the same since she'd found out about Glenn's stupid mistake with a lodger a year earlier. Even though she had stayed, there was a certain aloofness that Glenn supposed would now be permanent. They talked about the running of the farm and exchanged chat about their days, but that was the extent of it.

Still, there was always the pub. Home had a smell of guilt about it that Glenn could briefly drown in a pint glass.

Friday evening arrived, and there was Lewis, in a tattered Range Rover by the lower gate.

"There's an owl hole in the top barn," muttered Lewis as they made their way along the narrow country lane in the darkness, headlights sweeping the hedgerows.

"I didn't know barns still had those," Glenn replied.

"Old barn innit? Just grain in there now, fed in through a slide from a bucket. Plenty o' mice get in there, so the owl hole is still useful."

"Well, it might be, but it won't be big enough for us."

"For you," he said, and Glenn could tell by the volume that he'd turned to face him. "If he catches me in there, I'm sacked."

They remained silent for a while as the car rattled along the bumpy lane.

"And the deeds are in there?" Glenn said eventually.

"Yep, a part of it has some filing cabinets; a few old papers and stuff."

"Lewis?"

"Uh?"

"Why are you helping me?"

"Like I said, callous old fucker inn'e?"

The car stopped well before the farmhouse and they took to the fields with small torches to light the way. Lewis had picked a coil of rope and a small bag from the back of the car. Within a few minutes the hulking shape of the McAllister farmhouse came into relief against the inky night sky.

They crept by it, then past a series of outbuildings which framed the large yard.

"There," whispered Lewis as they arrived at the barn.

Glenn shone a torch up and picked out the owl hole, which was wide enough to get several bald eagles through. There was a plinth the birds would rest on, and beyond that the darkness of the barn.

"You know, having a key would have been easier," he whispered.

"He collects all the keys at the end o' day," replied Lewis. "He runs this place like a prison camp."

"Well, I'm not sure I can get up there."

"Course you fuckin' can. Look, I'm riskin' it doin' this with you. We shook on it, remember?"

Glenn didn't remember but could see that wouldn't cut any mustard. Lewis, though quiet, methodical and calculating, also had an element of randomness about him that scared Glenn slightly. He reminded him of the occasional nutcase you'd get in town, the type that, once you'd spoken to him, would follow you about and rant.

After a few minutes Lewis had looped the rope around the owl plinth and Glenn, using the undulating walls, had pulled himself up the side of the building. One more effort and he dropped inside, then scanned his surroundings with the torch.

He could have done with a brighter light in this barn. The torch just about picked out a bed of grain in the centre. There was a walled partition at the far end, with a frosted glass door. It appeared to be some sort of annex, as Lewis had suggested.

Inside was the filing cabinet, an old grey iron-clasped thing against the back wall. Glenn slid open the drawers one by one and, with grain dust assaulting his nostrils, started rifling through the papers.

The world went white with pain as he caught a flurry of movement.

Glenn floated. He circled around his house and saw Molly in every room. She was in her study, in her car, in the driveway and the kitchen. In their bed.

He looked out to the garden and saw her there, acting like she was playing with a child, only there was no one in front of her. "Ring a ring of roses," she sang, clasping hands with someone small and unseen.

He floated up, now high above the farm. There were versions of Molly everywhere. A memory of her by every hedge and bale. Patting the cows and astride the tractor.

He descended again, drifting past the roof, the guttering and top-floor windows, down past the ivy that had clambered over their farmhouse for decades, and to the ground.

And into the earth.

He was vertical, but his feet were driving down into the soil.

He still saw her playing with the child they didn't have.

He dropped lower, and higher rose the surrounding earth, the cold clamp of clay around his legs.

Still she played. Glenn shouted, unheard.

He was going underground now. He implored Molly not to leave.

~

Glenn came round.

There was a hissing, like a thousand snakes. A few low tungsten lightbulbs were now lit. The sound was grain, falling from a bucket high in the roof. The falling torrent pinned him as it clattered around his waist. He screamed for help.

"Ain't no help, misser," intoned Lewis from the other side of the barn door, his voice muffled through the old oak.

"What, what the fuck?"

"Worked here ten years, will work here thirty more. Master needs your farm dunn'e."

"My...what?"

"Shootin' yer mouth off to all every week. Your missus deserves better than that."

"Help!"

"Don't waste yer breath."

Glenn wriggled desperately, but to no avail. With each push, he sank further into the mounting barley.

Minutes later Lewis appeared to have gone, or had fallen silent, waiting for his victim to expire.

Glenn blinked away salt tears, as the grain rose gently above lips that would not get the chance to kiss Molly goodbye.

Snick

I drove past Tolmere Heath again last week.

From the road, one sees little more than a few scrubs of gorse. They are yellow-flowered in spring, and peek above the ancient anti-tank blocks, which now loll at odd angles like stone tortoises. It could be someone's  unrestricted back garden; you wouldn't know from a car. Walkers know this place though, whether they are dog-strollers or amblers. It continues to be popular, despite several unexplained disappearances down the years, about which the locals have some myths.

The heath stretches from the golf club pavilion in the north across an area of about fifteen square miles. Its eastern perimeter is the hot rod stadium car park, where every Sunday punters come from across town to breathe in gasoline and eat hot dogs covered with dust.

Farther south is the estate where I grew up and where my parents still live.

I will never set foot on the heath again for any length of time.

My love of the heath began as a child. After all, I am now a biologist of no little repute, and those formative years clanking my little bicycle around the impacted dirt paths and stony lanes of Tolmere filled me with a lasting love of nature.

My parents' house is close to the heath, only a fifteen-yard step to a bracken-gated pathway. Beyond consists mainly of scrub and stage-two heathland habitat. My memories of summer in the eighties are filled with butter-flies and dragonflies, soft silk webs across leaves, and the startled bounding of spooked squirrels. Although foxes mainly roamed near the refuse bins on the estate, they established their dens here, and on a lucky day you might catch a pair of jewelled eyes studying you from deep within a hedge.

The main expanse of the old golf course on the heath was laced with pathways, some hidden, some obvious. Curious places dotted the centre - a bicycle track, well before the BMX phenomenon, tree-studded banks littered with strange, fey hummocks, and a place we called 'The Maze'.

The Maze was the social epicentre of my fellow bike-obsessed childhood friends. We had no idea of its origin, but the result was a lattice of scrub-lined corridors covering a square kilometre, with the same bewildering, disorientating effect of any hand-crafted maze you might find at a stately home. We would congregate there on the summer weekends, split into loose teams and create arcane but exciting games, with scoring systems that would have been unfathomable to anyone older. We hurtled around the high-hedged pathways, sometimes passing one another, often colliding, but always having a blast. The expert maze riders would know when to hold their handle-bars in the centre rather than by the grips, lest gorse needles porcupine their sore fingers at the end of an action-filled day.

In time, we all grew up. Some friends moved away, others started seeing partners, and The Maze fell silent.

In later years I would return with my notepad and camera and explore the habitat differently. I wrote my PhD on the entomology of the heath, focusing on the rare butterfly species, and my wonder at the interconnectedness of the place only deepened. However, one area I could never fully study was The Maze.

It seemed simple enough but, in places, the thicket was so prohibitively dense that I could only speculate about the scurrying, fluttering and scampering going on within. I could study the paths and the outer layer of shrubs and plants but, in mapping the space out with a trisect and compass, a core patch of about fifty square yards was inaccessible.

It left me with a conundrum. The heath was officially owned by the sniffy golf course, who automatically turned down any request for alteration of their grounds. No one ever really came to The Maze, as it was away from the main pathways. With my peer generation all grown-up, an electronic spell had fallen upon the local youth. These days races and competitions were more commonplace behind the console-glowed lounge curtains of the estate than out there on the dirt tracks.

I rationalised that I could explore my way into the core of The Maze a little. Not enough to spoil an ancient habitat, but just enough to gain a narrow corridor of access to study the life within.

So, one summer on my return from studying at university, this is what I did together with Jackie.

Jackie. I imagine to many others I came across as a geek, and I admit to showing little interest in girls even during my freshers' year. Jackie was different. For a start, she was a brilliant botanist. She understood all the phases of plant growth, particularly deciduous woodland and heathland, and showed a rare aptitude for linking the fundamentals of zoology to the success of plant species. Some jocks and goons in my year joked that she wasn't 'a looker', with her mousey hair and pale face. To me she was enchanting. We shared coffee and chats late into the night in the university library. Before long we were dating when it didn't clash with our studies.

Jackie was at odds with her family, and so she asked if she could visit me over that summer at my parents' home. My mother said yes, delighted that I had found someone, and she charmed them from the off. I was happy she was with me, not only for company, but to help with the study of The Maze I planned to undertake in those weeks. Her science skills would be invaluable.

"The most important thing," I said as we approached it for the first time, "is to leave it all as it should be. We can cut through only so far as we need to, make notes and take photographs, but we shouldn't collect." Jackie was of the same frame of mind as me. Habitats should be sacrosanct and animals, be they bird, insect or worm, must be allowed to carry on as nature intended. This was the glory of life. Observation and recording should define zoology, not collection and pickling.

In time we had incised a tract of about ten feet into the heart of The Maze. Keeping low, we had worked in shifts, creating a mini tunnel that pushed beyond the first few rows of bushes. Progress had already thrown up some interesting discoveries, with layers of silkworm evidenced, and some fascinating ant-colony excavations clear on the arid topsoil. During my second rest, Jackie gave a little cry of excitement. I put down my flask of tea.

"Look at this!" she said, backing out of the clipped passage, hair mussed by branches. I went back in.

Several large webs spanned multiple plant roots. They had the classic structure of garden spider webs, a sort of crowning, spiralling neatness, but were larger than I had previously seen. One web, clearly a single structure, was nearly two feet across.

"Look at the parcelling," said Jackie behind me. The light was low here, as the gentle summer sun filtered through the layers of needles above. I saw what she meant. Most web spiders have a habit of injecting their prey with venom to pacify them, and then they spin a cocoon-like shroud around the immobile victim, to preserve them for later feasting. Several large flies were trussed up in this manner, but where normally you could see the whole insect parcelled whole, each of these large flies was limbless.

At that moment a frenetic buzzing sounded by my right

ear and, turning, I witnessed a freshly-caught greenbottle trapped and thrashing desperately upon one web.

And there! Forward crept the mistress! She was beautiful, and larger than any spider I had seen previously on the heath. Her brown body was solid and fat, and culminated in the tapering hourglass shape of a typical British garden spider. Her legs, however, were more like that of a house spider, thick and hairy. I held up a pen and measured her at about four inches, front leg to back. Her approach dwarfed the large fly.

"What's happening?" Jackie called. I shushed her.

"I'll tell you in a moment," I whispered, wanting to witness this ritual in its entirety. Forward edged the spider.

I had expected her to grab the fly with the ends of her legs, circle to the thorax and deliver a venomous bite, much as this class usually does. However, she surprised me. She reached out a single leg and patted the fly on one of its compound eyes. This prompted the insect to thrash with greater urgency as it sensed the mortal danger. The spider then reached forward to trace the underside of the thorax, and then, with her scything mandibles flexing - snick! - bit off a leg.

I had never seen such behaviour. I watched with a thrilled scientific fascination as this beautiful creature did her work. She moved around her hapless victim and severed each limb in turn, then moved to the wings and, with an almost imperceptible snick, removed those too. Before long, the fly was just an inert tube of dwindling life, mouthpiece twitching spasmodically, but no other means of movement possible. The spider then cast a light, lacy web about this ghastly banquet – nothing stronger was needed - before she crept back to her concealed resting place.

Upon exiting the tunnel, my description of this curious

encounter tumbled out. Jackie crept in and confirmed things as I had seen them. The day was drawing on, but we planned to come back each day for the rest of the week and finish our studies.

It would make for a superb summer research essay. I already imagined the praise from my tutor.

The rest of the week was exhausting but happy. My parents, sixties' night owls by nature, kept us occupied until the small hours after dinner, but by morning light we were back down at The Maze, extending the tunnel to see what more we could find.

Our last visit on the Friday uncovered a great surprise. At the very centre of The Maze the ground sloped away. It was hard to see completely from my cramped position, working with the shears, but what looked like a very large rabbit hole seemed to lie beyond the final few tiers of foliage. At first I thought it was darker soil but, no, it was a hole.

The next few hours revealed that the pit was larger than I had first thought. The mouth of it was in fact nearly eight feet across. Did the gorse take hold farther inside it? I hacked away at the thick roots until exhausted, then handed over to Jackie. I retreated to our station and took a minute to lie back and regain my energy.

All around me were the sounds of an English heathland summer. Blackbirds gently sang from the trees, and overhead a little single-engine plane buzzed its lazy way across a cerulean sky. The only other sound was the soft slicing of shears on roots as Jackie carried on with our work. I looked up at the single cloud visible in the sky and, ebbing with fatigue, imagined shapes. It was a boat.

No, a whale.

Maybe a rocket.

Perhaps ten minutes passed, maybe thirty, before I opened my eyes. A softness behind my eyes told me I'd briefly nodded off as the week's exertions took their toll on my less than athletic body. There was a blackbird still, with its sweet whistle. The plane had passed and the day seemed quieter.

"How are you getting on?" I called, to which there was no reply.

The light was dimmer, as the sun was now low on the horizon. I picked up our cheap electric torch and entered the little study tunnel, which by now was about twenty yards long.

As I reached the end, I saw that Jackie had finished the last cutting and had reached the hole. Peering over the side, I couldn't see the bottom. The sunlight, struggling as it did to penetrate this far into the thicket, stopped about a foot or two into the pit. I shone the torch down. It was deeper than I had imagined, with root-laced sides. The torchlight glinted off something that had to have been a full thirty feet down.

"Jackie?"

Was she injured? Had she fallen and knocked herself out? I climbed down, using roots to hold and step on.

On reaching the bottom, I saw that the metallic object was the pair of shears. The soil they lay on was soft and cold to the touch. The air had a sweet, sappy smell. I turned around a full 360 degrees and saw that the pit continued eastwards via a tunnel.

Snick. There was also another indistinct sound from

that direction. A voice? A light electric current passed over my skin.

I crouched and entered the mouth of the tunnel, which was just lower than my standing height.

Snick. Louder now. The tunnel broadened. The background sound grew louder, but undulated, like the lowing of a cow far away.

I passed into a chamber. The ceiling maintained more or less the same height as before, but the floor dropped away into a larger room-like cavity. My cheap torch strained to pick out the walls.

SNICK. The sound came from within this space! A sob. The background sound was a moan. With a grotesque, fleshy thump, a disembodied forearm dropped into the beam of the torch. I dropped it with a startled cry and it went out.

A muffled scream.

A loud tapping.

I scrambled to pick the torch up. At first the button didn't work, but with a couple of shakes it flickered back into life. I thrust it towards the wall.

Jackie was fixed to the surface by what looked like thick strands of glutinous rope, her face pinned against the wall. Hunched over her was an enormous arachnid shape, fully ten feet across, mandibles curved like sabres. Its legs tapped around Jackie's frame as her remaining leg pushed weakly against the webbing. Below, at the base of the wall, two arms and the other leg lay on the floor.

SNICK. Its final, horrific operation completed, I watched, repulsed, as the creature spun a light net of silk across Jackie's blonde hair. She turned her head slightly, and I caught the fading insane glint of her left eye as the webbing covered it over.

I scrambled away and fled screaming.

∼

By the time I reached home I knew that Jackie was dead. My parents were away that weekend, and it left me alone with my shock and terror. While I showered, anguished practical thoughts competed with my trauma. What should I do?

This was without doubt a discovery of immense value, but who would believe it? And if they did, what would happen? So often clumsy discoveries prove ruinous to species. For me it was always all about studying, not collection. What right did I have to bring disruption to this astonishing animal?

I cut the Gordian knot with a blade of pragmatism. The story was that Jackie had gone home. When the police eventually called, they found no sign that this wasn't true. Her parents said she had been unhappy at home, and after a few years the case was finally closed. They interviewed me a few times, but I had nothing further to add. They assumed that Jackie had just upped sticks and moved abroad.

Occasionally I visit my parents, but I no longer go to the heath. At night, once the larks have finished their daily exertions, only the odd screech of a tawny owl carries across the bush-tops to the spare room where I lie.

Sometimes I figure I might just hear a short, soft sound carried on the night air.

Snick.

About the Author

Paul Draper is writer and filmmaker. He produces screenplays as well as prose fiction. He is a bit of a lefty as many of his type are, but he only wants the best for everyone really. He feeds birds on his balcony and loves cats.

Connect with Paul

www.twitter.com/theblackgate
www.instagram.com/blackgatesight
www.facebook.com/itstheblackgate
email: p@uldraper.co.uk

More books coming soon.